WALT DISNEY
PICTURES PRESENTS

Pooh's Heffalump MOVIE

Ladybird

One honey-sunny morning, deep in the Hundred-Acre Wood, a strange noise bellowed and trumpety-rumpetied through the trees. It woke everyone up!

From his window, Roo watched as a very anxious Tigger, Pooh and Piglet rushed through the wood. They looked like they had left home in a great hurry, and they seemed very frightened.

"Where's everybody going?" called Roo.

"To Rabbit's house," said Piglet. "He'll know what to do!"

Roo raced after his friends.

While the others told Rabbit about the sound, Roo spotted a giant footprint. Everyone had a look – including Eeyore, who was wandering by.

Rabbit thought the only thing that could have made such a huge footprint was a heffalump!

Published by Ladybird Books Ltd.
A Penguin Company
Penguin Books Ltd, 80 Strand, London WC2R 0RL

Penguin Books Australia Ltd, Camberwell, Victoria, Australia
Penguin Group (NZ), cnr Airborne and Rosedale Roads, Albany,
Auckland 1310, New Zealand

1 3 5 7 9 10 8 6 4 2

"What's a heffalump?" asked Roo.

"It's got fiery eyes and a tail with a spike!" said Tigger, with a shudder.

"Heffalumps are terribly hazardous," added Rabbit. "They live right over there in Heffalump Hollow."

Suddenly a trumpeting sound echoed around them. It was the heffalump!

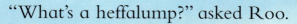

"Let's go get him!" cried Roo excitedly.
"It'll be fun!"

Rabbit agreed. "Come back with your
equipment," he told everyone, "and I'll
show you how it's done!"

A little later, everyone returned with all
sorts of bits and pieces to help capture
the heffalump. Roo was the only one to
bring anything useful – some rope.

They practised by trying to capture a barrel. Rabbit told everyone to take aim and say, "In the name of the Hundred-Acre Wood, I capture you!" Roo was the only one who managed it. "I did it! I did it!" he cried.

But Rabbit thought the expedition would be very dangerous. "You're too young," he explained to Roo.

Poor Roo trudged home. How he
wished he were grown up!

"You're growing up very fast, dear,"
Kanga assured him. She knew that
growing up takes its own time.

But Roo didn't want to wait. Early the next day, taking his rope, he set off alone for Heffalump Hollow.

Rabbit and the others were heading off too.

"Remember," Rabbit said, "the important thing is that we stick together."

But somehow Pooh and Piglet ended up taking the wrong path.

In the hollow, Roo met something. The something said he was called Lumpy . . . and that he was a heffalump. Roo thought he seemed very friendly, and not horribly hazardous at all.

"I have to capture a heffalump," said Roo flinging his rope around Lumpy's neck. Lumpy cheered, and tried to trumpet. "I haven't found my call yet," he explained.

Roo wanted to take Lumpy back to meet Rabbit and the others, but when they reached the Hundred-Acre Wood, Lumpy stopped.

"I'm not supposed to go into that part of the wood," he said. "Scary things live there!"

"That's where I live," said Roo, "and my friends. There aren't any scary things there, I promise!"

The Hundred-Acre Wood was quiet when Lumpy and Roo got there. Lumpy was very hungry so they made their way to Pooh's house for some delicious honey, and then to Rabbit's garden for some yummy watermelon.

The very best thing to do after a meal of sticky honey and messy melon is to head for a cooling swim, followed by lots of running around to dry off, so that's just what they did.

But Roo thought it would be much
easier to play if Lumpy didn't have
a rope around his neck.

"You're not captured any more,"
he said.

Lumpy had become his friend.

At about the same time, Pooh, Piglet, Tigger and Rabbit headed for home.

"A successful heffalump expedition!" Rabbit announced. "There are no heffalumps about!"

Then they noticed the footprints leading to Pooh's house and Rabbit's garden. The friends followed them and gasped when they saw the broken pots and honey puddles in Pooh's house. The mess in Rabbit's garden was even worse.

"The heffalumps are among us!" cried
Rabbit. "We need traps!"

They used everything they could find
to build some very big and frightening
heffalump traps.

"Now," said Rabbit in a frightening
voice, "to await the attack!"

Lumpy and Roo were still playing when they heard a heffalump calling from far away. It was Lumpy's mum.

"She sounds worried," said Lumpy. "I'd better go."

But the more the two friends searched, the farther away Lumpy's mum seemed to be. And with every step, Lumpy missed her more and more.

Roo tried to cheer him up by singing his favourite song – the one Kanga sang. Now they both missed their mums!

"Let's go back and find my mum," Roo said.

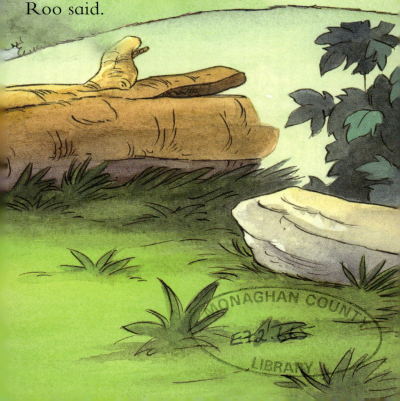

Just over the hill, Roo spotted Kanga with Pooh, Piglet, Rabbit and Tigger.

"Mum!" he called, rushing to her.

"Roo!" Kanga answered happily. She had been worried about him.

Roo introduced Lumpy to everyone. "He's a heffalump!" Roo said proudly.

"A heffalump!" shouted Rabbit. "And it's got Roo!"

"Stop him!" yelled Tigger.

Lumpy was terrified and ran away, but he hadn't gone far when he was caught in the huge heffalump trap!

Roo rushed to help his new friend. "I'll get you out!" he cried.

He had to work quickly. Scrambling to the top of the cage, Roo untied the knot holding it together, and Lumpy was free!

"C'mon!" Roo hugged his friend. "Let's get you back home."

But the others soon caught up and, thinking Roo was in danger, were determined to capture Lumpy with their ropes.

"In the name of the Hundred-Acre Wood," shouted the rescue squad, "I capture you!" Could brave little Roo save his friend again?

"Stop!" cried Roo. "Lumpy's my friend. Heffalumps aren't big and scary – he's just a kid like me!"

Roo explained that sometimes Lumpy got frightened, just like Piglet. And that he liked honey, just like Pooh. "He's even learning to bounce," he told Tigger. "You gotta uncapture him!"

One by one, Piglet, Pooh, Tigger – and even Rabbit – dropped their ropes.

But Lumpy was still scared, and as he tried to run away, he fell down a steep slope. Roo tried to stop him falling, and tumbled down a big hole himself.

Everyone gasped. How could they rescue poor Roo? But Lumpy knew exactly what to do. Lifting his trunk, he trumpeted, "TAROOT! TAROOT!" Lumpy had found his call at last!

Far in the distance, another trumpet replied, and soon Mama Heffalump crashed into the clearing.

"I've been worried sick," she said, hugging Lumpy.

"I'm okay, Mummy," said Lumpy, "but my friend Roo's in trouble."

"Leave it to me," she said.

Using her trunk, Mama Heffalump gently pulled Roo out of the hole, and at last everyone was reunited.

Now Pooh understood. "The heffalump was looking for her baby," he told Rabbit. "That's why she was in the wood!" Rabbit knew Pooh was right, and said sorry to Lumpy for trying to capture him.

"That's okay, Long Ears," said Lumpy, forgiving his brand-new friend.

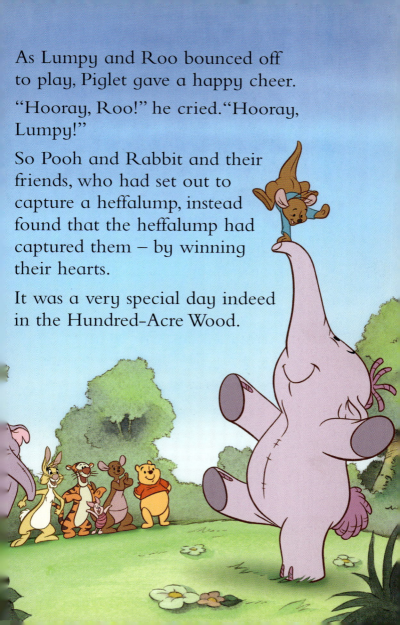

As Lumpy and Roo bounced off to play, Piglet gave a happy cheer.

"Hooray, Roo!" he cried. "Hooray, Lumpy!"

So Pooh and Rabbit and their friends, who had set out to capture a heffalump, instead found that the heffalump had captured them – by winning their hearts.

It was a very special day indeed in the Hundred-Acre Wood.